The Mystery of Porpoise Point

Mike Holliday

FishingKids
White Bear Lake, Minnesota

The Mystery of Porpoise Point

FishingKids
PO Box 10590,
White Bear Lake, MN 55110
www.fishingkids.com

Library of Congress Control Number: 2011942335

Credits

Cover and Interior Illustrations
Olga and Aleksey Ivanov

Spinner's Notebook Sketches and Map
Marilyn Emma Anderson

Creative Direction
Megan Derbes McCarthy

Layout and Design
Flat Sole Studio

Printed in the United States of America in Stevens Point, Wisconsin

Table of Contents

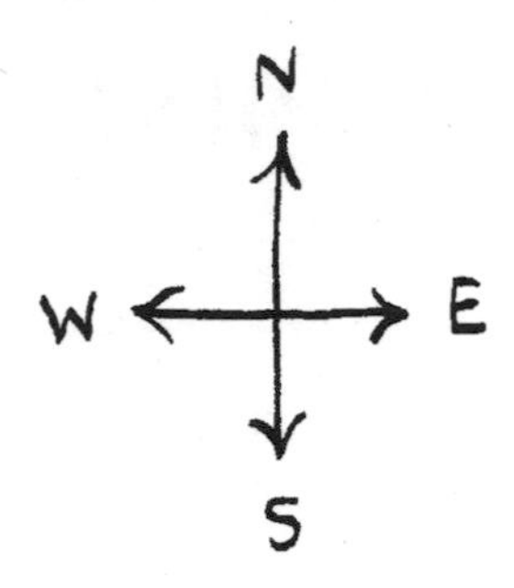

Islamorada, Florida

Campground
Cheeca Rocks
Reef

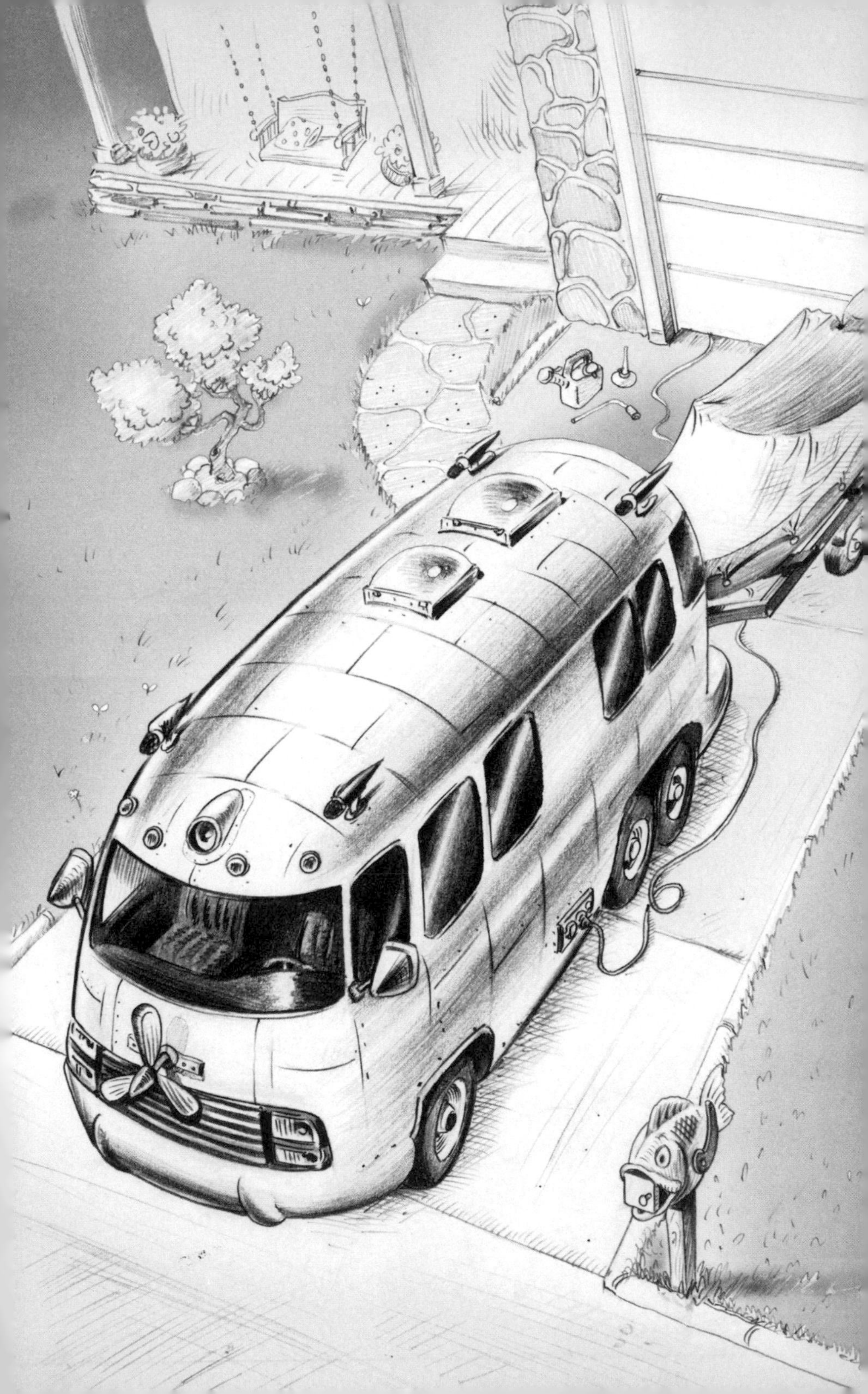

Prologue

The Chief, Bobber, and I were in the garage putting some line on a spinning reel when Uncle Pete walked up. The Chief has two sons — my dad, who is an engineer, and my Uncle Pete, who used to be a pilot but is now retired. He recently bought a recreational vehicle and a boat so he could travel around the country.

An RV is like a big camper with an engine. You can drive wherever you want to go and bring all your gear from home. It may take longer to drive somewhere than to fly there by plane, but Uncle Pete says it's better because you get to see the country and meet new people.

The Zephyr — Uncle Pete's nickname for his RV — is not just any recreational vehicle. It's all silver like a big bullet with wheels, with black tinted windows all around, and mounted on the front is a big wooden propeller that spins when we get going real fast. He says the Zephyr is his airplane on wheels.

When he first bought it, Uncle Pete and my dad spent two weeks modifying the Zephyr. They put in satellite TV, an Internet connection, a satellite phone, GPS, and a camera on the back so Uncle Pete could look at the monitor and see what's behind him.

About a week ago, The Chief told me that Uncle Pete was going on a fishing trip to the Florida Keys, and he wanted us to come along. I almost jumped out of my pants with excitement. I haven't been able to sleep the last three nights waiting for this day to come. My dad has to work, so my friend Bobber's going take his place.

I did some research on the Florida Keys at the White Bear Lake Public Library. They start at the tip of Florida, next to the Florida Everglades, and go southwest all the way to Key West.

The Keys are closer to the equator than where I live in White Bear Lake, Minnesota, so the sun is stronger and the weather is warmer. They don't get snow, not even in winter. The water is warm and clear, because it flows through the islands from offshore.

The islands of the keys are small — usually less than a mile or two wide and 20 miles long. The Gulf of Mexico is on one side and the Atlantic Ocean is on the other. The Chief says you can watch the sun rise over the ocean in the morning, and then walk across the street and watch it set over the Gulf at night.

Uncle Pete says we're going to drive all the way to Islamorada, which is one of the islands of the Upper Keys. It has a huge campground and a beach. Islamorada is known for shallow water flats fishing and offshore fishing. I can't wait to do both. I hope we get to go snorkeling, too. I've got my mask and snorkel packed, and am ready to go.

I'll also bring my FishingKids Notebook. It was a Christmas gift from The Chief, and I use it to write down all the cool fishing stuff that he tells me. That way I won't forget anything.

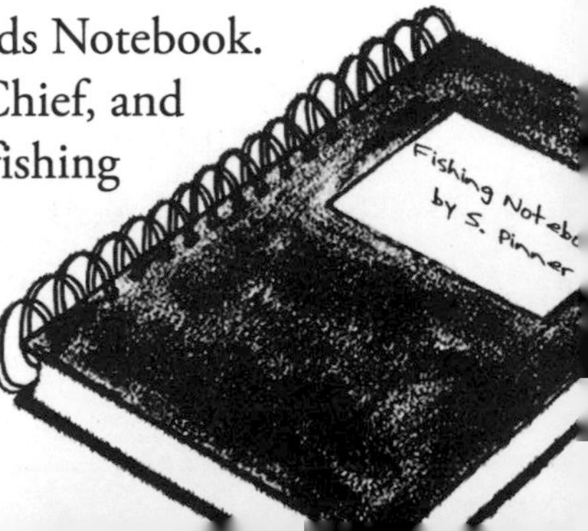

Now we just have to get our fishing rods ready. The Chief says we'll need lots of line on our reels because saltwater fish get bigger than most freshwater fish. I can't wait to catch a giant tarpon or bonefish, or even a mahi or sailfish!

Chapter 1

Lobster Heads

"Are you guys ready to go to the Keys?" asked Uncle Pete as he walked up to us holding a dive mask and snorkel.

Like The Chief and my dad, Uncle Pete is tall. He has red hair that's starting to turn gray, which he says is from "too many close calls while flying." He also has this way of smiling and winking that makes you feel like he's letting you in on some secret.

Although Uncle Pete is tall, he's a lot thinner than The Chief, with ginormous hands and feet. He says they help him swim like a fish. It must be true, because he can outswim just about everyone on White Bear Lake.

"It's been a long time since I've been down to Islamorada," said Uncle Pete. "Lobster season opened last week. We can go snorkeling and catch some for dinner."

"Lobster! That's awesome, Uncle Pete," I said. "But don't they pinch?"

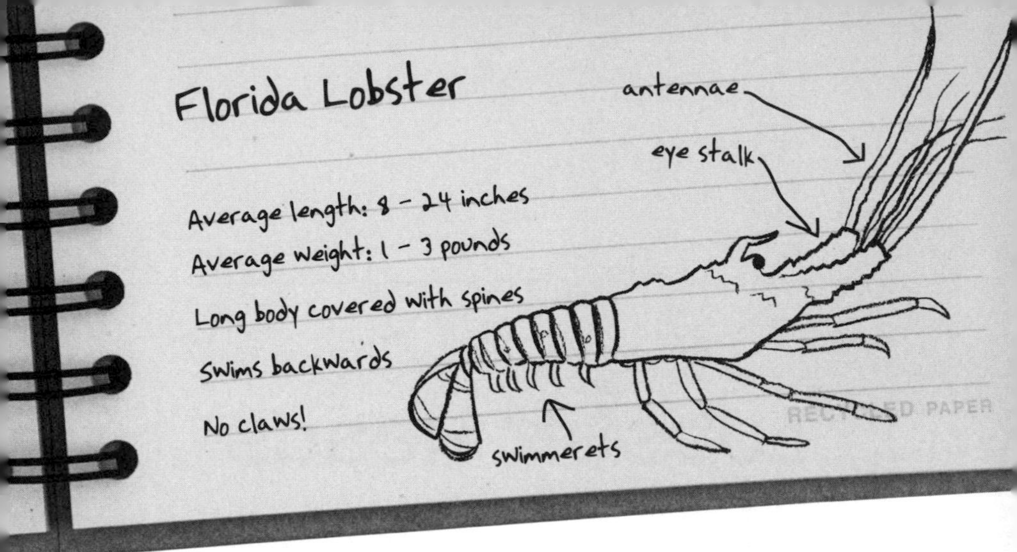

Uncle Pete smiled and winked, and then explained that Florida lobster don't have claws like northern lobster. They have two antennas that they use to grab their food and put it in their mouths. They are spiny though, so we'll need gloves.

The Chief went into one of the garage cabinets and got out three pairs of thick cloth gloves, along with a mesh bag to put the lobsters in.

"This should do," he said, putting the gloves in the bag. "Most of the shallow reefs are less than 10 feet deep, Spinner, but if you have problems diving down and grabbing the lobster, then you can hold the bag while I put the lobsters in it. We'll work as a team."

"I want to be on Uncle Pete's team," said Bobber. "We're gonna need a float to keep the bag from sinking or swimming away because of all lobsters and flounder we'll have in it."

"Um, they don't have a lot of flounder in the Keys," I said, knowing Bobber remembered flounder from the FishingKids Saltwater Gamefish Identification Cards my dad bought me. "But they do have tarpon, and bonefish, and sailfish, and snapper."

“Then I’ll snorkel like a super-cool-RV-diving-lobster-catching-tarpon-snapper!” he declared. Yep, having Bobber along was definitely going to add some extra fun to this trip.

Bobber and I helped The Chief and Uncle Pete carry the gear out to the Zephyr. When we got to the RV, it was obvious Uncle Pete had made some more changes. On the roof were two big plastic bubbles, and when we opened the door and looked inside, there was a metal ladder going up to the bubbles with seats mounted from the ceiling.

“Wow,” said Bobber, “RV forts.”

“Something like that,” said Uncle Pete with a smile and a wink. “The best part about flying was having the wind in my face, so if I get too cooped up in the RV, I can climb up the ladder, sit down, and open the bubble canopy. I have pilot’s goggles in the seats to make it seem like you’re flying.”

Bobber and I stared in amazement. The Zephyr had to be the coolest RV in the world. I couldn’t wait to climb the ladder and stick my head out all the way to Florida. I did have one concern though.

“I’ve never caught a lobster, Chief,” I said as I put our fishing gear in the storage area down below.

“It’s pretty easy. You simply grab them with your hands,” he said. “Just keep an eye open for sharks, or moray eels, or barracuda, or any of the other creatures that might also be on the reef.”

“Sharks? There are sharks?” I said with a gulp, thinking about swimming with man-eating sharks. “And moray eels and barracuda?”

Chapter 2

Itchy to Explore

Along with the television and a DVD player, Uncle Pete's RV has a computer. Bobber and I spent a lot of the time on the drive to the Keys looking up lobsters and different kinds of Florida fish on the Internet.

It took almost two days of driving to get to Islamorada. Bobber and I also spent a lot of time riding in the pilot's seats with the bubble open and our goggles on. We pretended we were flying down the highway in an amphibious boat-plane.

We knew we were getting close to the Florida Keys when we went over a bridge, and the water was turquoise like a big blue river. We could smell the salt in the air and see that the trees grew out of the water and had huge roots. The Chief said they were mangroves, and that juvenile fish lived in safety among their roots.

Uncle Pete pulled the Zephyr into the Islamorada RV Park. The park ranger showed us where our campsite was. It was right on the water with a beach in front of it.

The Zephyr has air brakes that hiss and blow out air when you stop. When we pulled into the camp site, it let out a loud *WHOOOOOSH!*, which sounded like it was saying, "Whew," after the long trip and was happy to rest.

While Uncle Pete and The Chief secured the Zephyr and plugged in the electric and water, Bobber and I walked down to the beach and put our feet in the salt water. It felt stickier than the water in White Bear Lake.

Along the shore the sand was hard, but it got softer the farther out we went. Mixed with the sand was turtlegrass, a wide-bladed grass that grew about a foot high from the bottom. Wherever the turtlegrass was, the sand was so soft we would sink up to our knees.

"Holy quicksand!" said Bobber as he sank past his knees. "It's a man-eating saltwater salad!"

Bobber took a step, pulling his foot from the sandy mud.

SCHLOOP!

He took another step.

SCHLOOP!

Every time Bobber pulled his foot out of the soft sand, the suction made a schlooping noise. Then when he put it back down, he sunk quietly into the sand.

We schlooped along for a while before we finally got to a shallow sand bar where the sand was harder and we didn't sink. There was a girl about our age standing on the sandbar skipping shells. She had brown hair and a straw hat the size of Minnesota.

She was super tan and had a backpack on, and long fishing shorts that looked like the pockets were stuffed with sea shells. She looked over at us and smiled.

"You guys are walking in itch mud," said the girl. "There are little organisms in there that sting your skin. Then it makes you itch later."

"Itch mud?" I said. "I'm not itching."

"That's because you're still in the water. When you get out and dry off, you'll sure feel it," she said.

"That's probably just your cooties that itch," said Bobber, who then began to explain his theory about girls. "Every girl has cooties. That's why girls smell like flowers, and why they like school and doing chores and playing dress up. They've got cooties, which probably also make their legs itch."

"Um, Bobber, I think she might be right," I interrupted. "My legs are kind of starting to itch."

"Yeah, well, you probably got too close and got some of her . . ." Bobber's voice trailed off and his eyes went down to his legs. "Hey, mine are starting to itch, too," he said.

Bobber started running for shore.

"I've got girl cooties on my legs! I've got the itch mud girly leg cooties!"

Just then, The Chief and Uncle Pete walked out of the RV. They looked at each other and smiled. The Chief turned on the hose and motioned for Bobber to come over.

"Now, boys, you aren't giving that nice girl a hard time, are you? It's just itch mud," said The Chief as he sprayed fresh water on our feet, ankles, and legs. "It'll stop in a minute. Try to walk only on the hard sand."

It didn't take long for the itching to stop. But the worst itching and scratching was still yet to come.

Chapter 3

Mosquito Bait

By late afternoon, everything was unpacked, and Uncle Pete decided it was time to put the boat in. We drove the RV to a boat ramp, and The Chief, Bobber, and I helped guide the RV as Uncle Pete backed the boat into the water. The Zephyr let out a loud *WHOOSH!* as it came to a stop, and we knew it was glad to not be pulling the boat any longer.

Uncle Pete's boat was a 22-foot Lowe aluminum V-hull with a 90-horsepower outboard motor. The silver color matched the Zephyr perfectly, and Uncle Pete had taken a paintbrush and painted the name *Water Zephyr* on the back. The Chief unhooked the boat from the trailer, and it floated off.

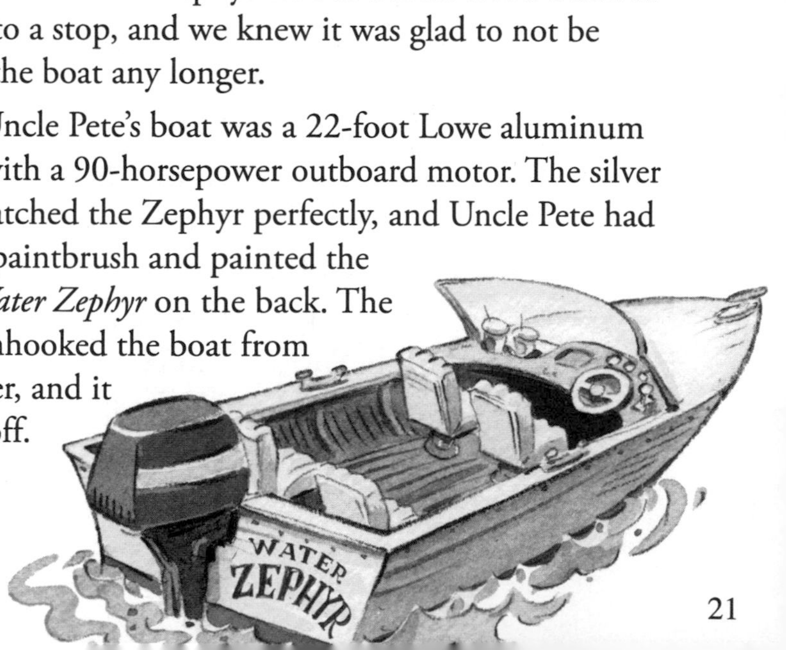

We got in the boat with The Chief, while Uncle Pete drove the RV back to the campsite. He then started the engine, and the *Water Zephyr* came to life.

"We're going to anchor the boat off the beach so we can wade out and use the boat whenever we want," said The Chief.

"Wow, it's like a giant dockless marina," said Bobber.

The Chief smiled and said, "There is a marina at the campground, right next to the Ranger's house, but something has been eating all the bait out of the buckets, so we'll put the boat where we can watch it."

To get back to the Islamorada campground, we had to go to the other side of the island, which meant we went under a bridge where the water was green and deep. When we got close to the campground, we saw the beach, the RV, and the seagrass beds.

"The shallow areas are called 'flats,'" explained The Chief. "That's where the grass grows and fish like bonefish, tarpon, and permit like to dig in the sand and grass for shrimp and crabs. It's usually less than two feet deep on the grass flats."

"Are bonefish the ones that look like giant suckers?" I asked The Chief, remembering the different Florida fish Bobber and I found on the Internet.

"They look a lot like suckers, but they're all silver with a black back. They're as fast as lightning when you hook them. Bonefish swim in schools, and their tails stick up out of the water when they feed," said The Chief as he motored slowly into the shallows and then threw out the anchor.

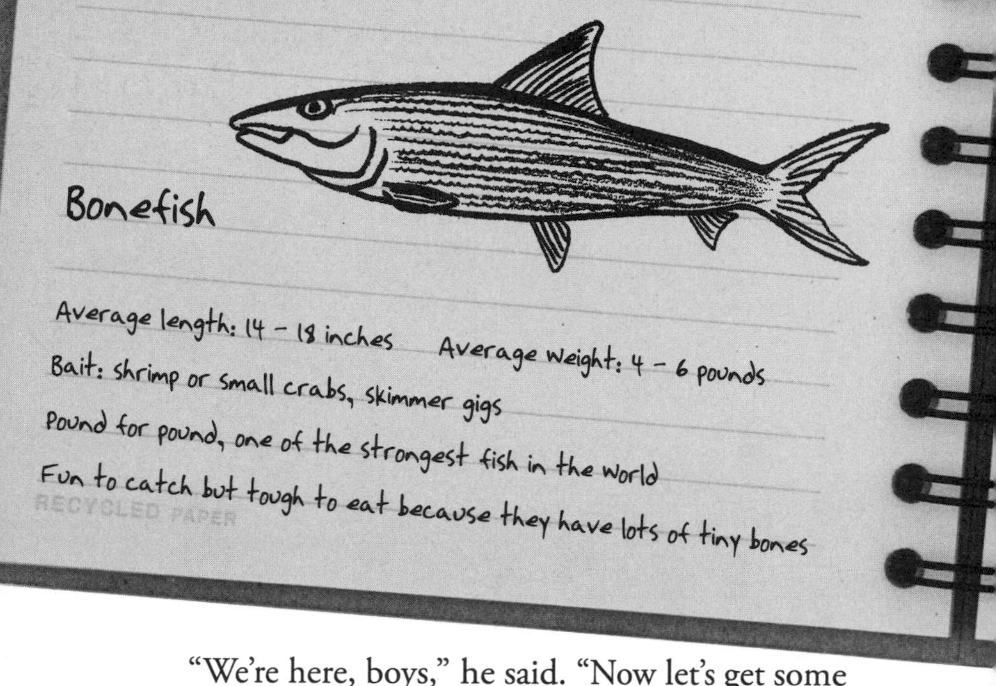

"We're here, boys," he said. "Now let's get some dinner started, so we can get back inside before the mosquitoes come out."

We all waded back to shore, making sure we walked on the sand and not the grass and itch mud. Back at shore, Uncle Pete had put charcoal in the grill and was pulling out a pack of hot dogs when we walked up.

"Oh, boy, hot dogs. My favorite," said Bobber as he licked his lips and started doing a dance and singing the hot dog song.

Hot dogs, hot dogs, cook them on the grill.
Hot dogs, hot dogs, eat them at your will.
Hot dogs, hot dogs, they're number one.
Hot dogs, hot dogs, put them on a bun!

That's the great thing about having Bobber as a best buddy. You never know what he's going to do or say next.

We had hot dogs, potato salad, and baked beans, and we ate until our bellies were just about to burst.

It was starting to get dark, and all the campers were turning on their lights. I was cleaning the dishes when that girl from the sandbar walked up and introduced herself. She looked a lot different from most girls I know, with that big straw hat covering her head and one long braided strand of hair with a fishing lure on the end.

"Hi," she said. "My name's Coral. My dad's a park ranger here. Where are you guys from?"

"White Bear Lake, Minnesota," I replied, noticing that Coral also had beads in her long hair. "About two days away."

"Do you have Native American Indians in White Bear Lake?" she asked. "I'm part Seminole Indian. They lived mainly in Florida."

"White Bear Lake was named for a Chippewa brave who killed a bear," I said. "The Okibway, Sioux, and Chippewa used to come there to make syrup. But that was a long time ago."

"We don't see a lot of kids here," said Coral. "It sure is nice to have someone to hang out with. Do you guys know how to fish?"

"We're the muskie champs of White Bear Lake," Bobber piped in with a smile. "We're here to catch tarpon, and lobsters, and anything else that swims."

"That's cool. We have lots of them around the Keys," said Coral. "We also have sharks, barracuda, moray eels, stingrays, snapper, and tuna. Islamorada is a great place to fish."

Coral told us she lived with her mom and dad at the Ranger Station on Porpoise Point, which was on the south end of the island. I wasn't sure which direction was south, so I pulled out my FishingKids compass and looked.

Right about then, my legs started to itch again. I looked down and saw about 10 mosquitoes on my feet and legs. From the look on his face, Bobber must have noticed the itching at the same time.

"Ahhh . . . they're flying mini blood-sucking pterodactyls!" he started yelling as he bent over and started scratching madly at his legs.

The mosquitoes were everywhere. Bobber was scratching his legs, back, and head, and waving his hands frantically in the air.

"It's just mosquitoes, Bobber!" I yelled. "We need to get inside."

All three of us went into the RV where Uncle Pete and The Chief were looking at a map of Long Island displayed on the big screen TV. Bobber and I were itching like mad, but Coral was acting normal, like she didn't even feel the mosquito bites.

"Haven't you guys ever heard of mosquito repellent?" asked Coral, shaking her head at us. "The Keys are part mangrove swamp, and the mosquitoes live in there by the millions. Geez, if you can't figure out how to use mosquito repellent, you won't be catching any saltwater fish while you're here."

"At White Bear Lake, our mosquitoes are big as eagles," said Bobber. "Every time a dog goes missing, we need to check to see if the mosquitoes were bad that day. And we're the best fishermen in Minnesota! I don't think Florida is going to be much of a challenge for us."

We introduced Coral to Uncle Pete and The Chief. She showed them on the map where the reef was and how to get to it using the channel to avoid the shallow flats. Then she said she had to go home.

"Before you go, Coral, what's the story with all the bait vanishing at the marina?" asked The Chief.

"Something is eating it out of the buckets at night," explained Coral. "You go to bed with a bait bucket full of shrimp and pinfish, and in the morning, it's gone. It's a big mystery. Some people think its otters opening the buckets and eating the fish, but we don't have any otters on Islamorada."

"So the buckets are still there, just empty in the morning?" said The Chief.

"Yep. But if you leave your fish on a stringer, they're gone, and the stringer is usually gone or busted. It's a crazy mystery that no one seems to know the answer to," said Coral.

"Well, guys, gotta fly," said Coral, holding her hand to her forehead like a salute. Then straightening her arm, she zipped out the door like her hand was an airplane pulling her along behind it.

"I like her already," said Uncle Pete.

"Interesting girl," said The Chief. "She sure knows a lot about The Keys."

Chapter 4

Tickled to Death

The next morning, Uncle Pete and The Chief were up early making breakfast and getting the boat ready for a day on the water. While Bobber and I ate breakfast, Uncle Pete told us about catching lobster.

"Florida lobster are really crawfish," he said. "They hide in holes in the coral reef, and you have to tickle them out using this stick. Then you catch them in the net and bring them to the surface."

The tickle stick was a fiberglass rod about two feet long and as thick as the top of a fishing pole.

Bobber had a strange look on his face. "Do lobsters have feet?" he asked.

"No Bobber, they have ten legs and long whiplike antennas, but no feet," said Uncle Pete.

"Then how do you tickle them?" asked Bobber.

"You don't really tickle them like you would to make someone laugh," explained Uncle Pete. "You gently tap them on the tail with the tickle stick. That makes them move forward and come out of the reef. Then you put the net over them."

In no time, we were finished with breakfast. We put our swim suits on and waded out to the boat. The Chief started the engine and headed for the reef. On the way out, we passed Coral's house on Porpoise Point.

On the run out, I saw a metal structure in the distance. I pointed it out to The Chief. The structure was shaped like a triangle, with thick, rusty metal beams welded together. It had a big black top with glass all around it and a metal roof. It looked like it had been there forever.

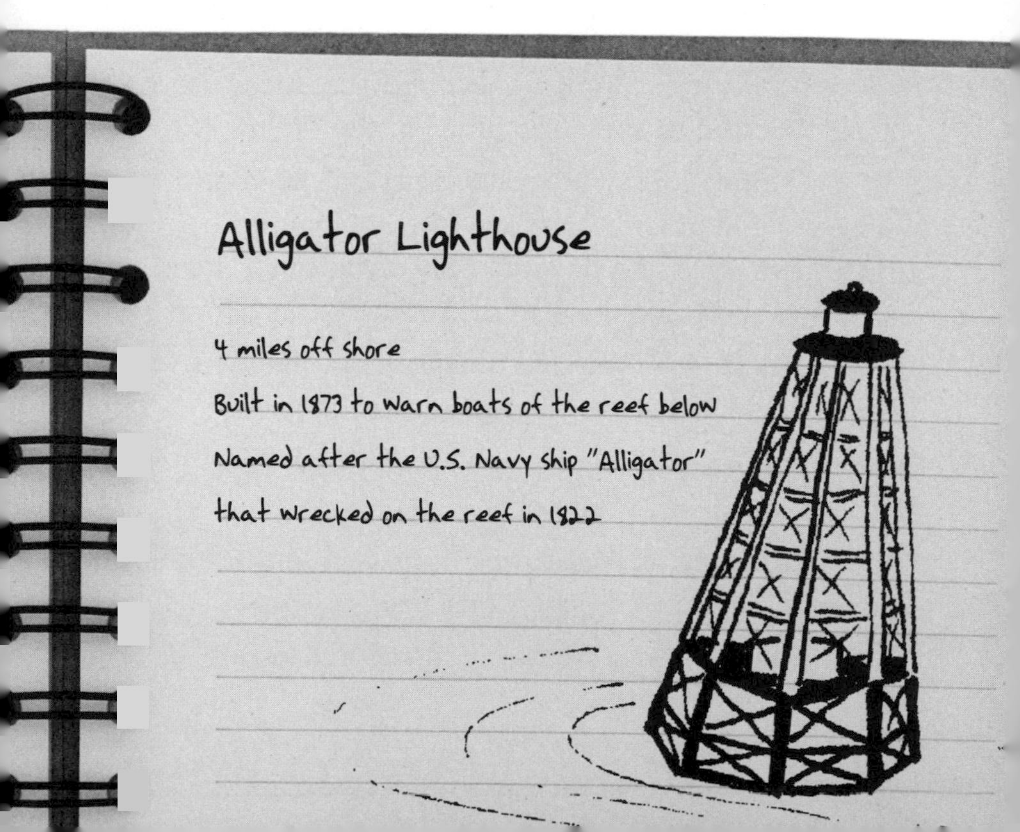

"That's Alligator Lighthouse," said The Chief. "The reef we're going to dive is right nearby, but outside the marine sanctuary."

"I'm not going in the water if there are alligators," announced Bobber. "They're way worse than mosquitoes."

"There are no alligators there, Bobber," said The Chief as we neared the lighthouse. The rusting metal stretched down into the clear water. "The lighthouse was named after the *USS Alligator,* a ship that wrecked on the reef. Plus, alligators like freshwater, not the Atlantic Ocean."

We anchored within sight of the lighthouse in water that was eight to ten feet deep. The water was so clear you could see the bottom.

Uncle Pete put up a dive flag, and we all put on our masks, snorkels, and fins and jumped in. The water was warm, and there were fish everywhere! Fish of all shapes and colors swam over the reef. Bobber and I stayed close to Uncle Pete and The Chief.

As we swam over a large section of reef, Uncle Pete grabbed my arm and pointed to a hole in the reef. Sticking out of the reef were dark red antennas about a foot long.

Uncle Pete took a deep breath and dove down to the reef, kicking his fins as he went. The Chief, Bobber, and I watched as Uncle Pete stuck his tickle stick in the hole. A lobster scooted out of the opening. Uncle Pete quickly put his net over it. Then he swam up to the surface.

"Open your bag, Spinner," said Uncle Pete. "This one's about two pounds. There are several more in that hole."

Uncle Pete put the lobster in the bag, and I pulled the drawstring tight. Then he dove back down and tickled another lobster out of the hole. In a short time, we had a bag completely full of Florida spiny lobsters.

On the ride back to Islamorada, I thought about the disappearing bait and busted fish stringers. Bobber and I were going to have to look further into the mystery when we got back to shore.

Chapter 5

What's the Porpoise of Life

When we arrived back at the campground, Coral was kneeling on the shoreline sticking what looked like big green beans into the sand. She watched us wade in from the boat. Uncle Pete carried the lobsters, and The Chief carried all our dive gear.

When we walked up, Coral saw the lobsters. She stopped what she was doing, stood up, and smiled.

"What are those long beans you're sticking in the sand?" I asked, pointing to the row of six or seven of them near her feet.

"They're mangrove seeds," Coral answered. "The trees drop them, and they float around with the tides, eventually ending up along the shorelines. If you put them in the sand, a mangrove will grow and provide a place for young fish to live," said Coral.

"You guys did great," she added, pointing to the lobsters. "If you need a place to clean them, we have a big fish cleaning table on the dock behind our house. You can catch snapper there, too."

Uncle Pete said he'd clean the lobsters and have the tails ready to put on the grill for dinner, but that it sure would be nice to have some fish to go with them. Bobber and I were quick to offer to go to Coral's house and catch some.

The Chief grabbed a bait bucket and walked over to the marina. He bought some shrimp while Bobber and I got our fishing rods ready to catch snapper. I took out my FishingKids Notebook and looked at the snapper rig The Chief had told us about.

We use 12-pound line, with a 30-inch 20-pound monofilament leader tied on using a uni-knot. On the other end of the leader we tied a loop knot to a 1/0 bait hook. We put two split shots at the top of the leader to help make the shrimp sink to the bottom where the snappers were hiding in the rocks.

Then Bobber and I grabbed the bait bucket and our fishing rods and walked down to Porpoise Point. Coral was sitting on the dock fishing when we got there.

"Catch anything?" asked Bobber, and from the tone of his voice, I could tell he was not expecting a girl to catch much. After all, she wasn't a muskie champ of White Bear Lake.

"Just a couple of big snapper," she smirked as she pointed to the rope stringer tied to the dock.

Bobber and I looked down, and there in the water were three red and gray snappers with black stripes on their bodies and a slanted dark stripe on their faces, all hanging on a rope stringer. Each of them probably weighed about two pounds.

"Geez, snapper fishing must be easy if a girl can catch them," said Bobber as he hooked a shrimp and tossed out his line. "I'm going to catch about 400 billion of them so you can see why only boys should do the

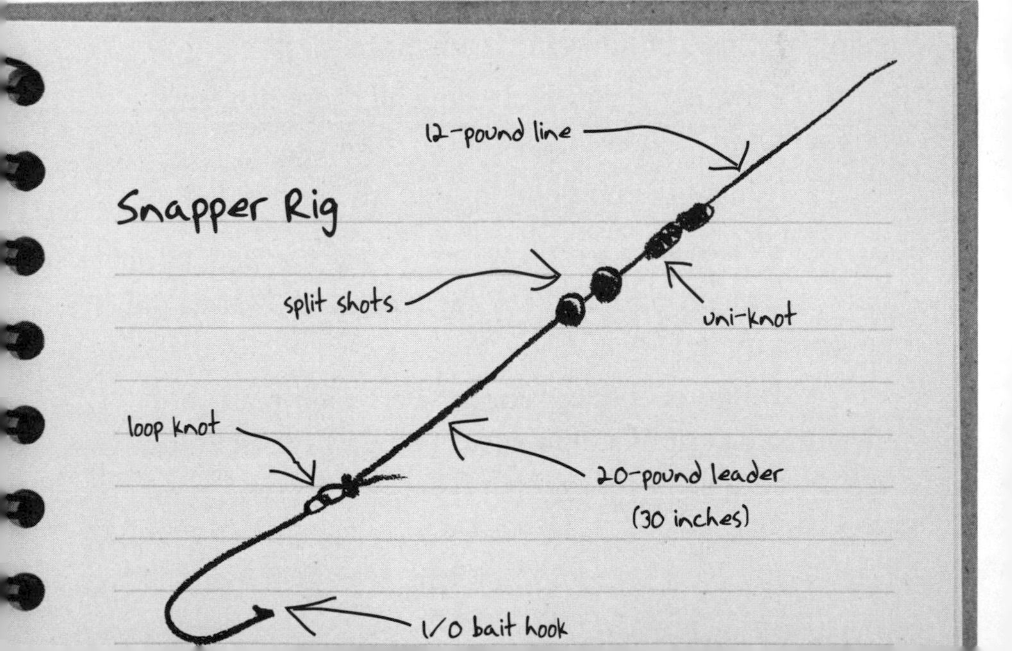

fishing around here. Didn't you know that girls aren't supposed to like slimy worms and stinky fish and sharp hooks?"

Coral stared hard at Bobber. Then she tipped her hat at us, smiled, and said, "Okay, Minnesota boys, it's on! Let me show you what a Florida girl can do."

She immediately got a bite, set the hook, and reeled in another two-pounder, which she then slid onto the rope stringer while smiling extra long at Bobber.

That made Bobber try even harder. He asked me to help him prove that girls aren't supposed to go fishing. We baited up with shrimp and cast to the snapper we could clearly see swimming around the dock.

In an hour of fishing, Bobber and I caught . . . nothing. Coral, on the other hand, caught three more snapper, one of which she said was too small and let go. The others she added to the stringer.

We couldn't believe it. Bobber and I were getting beat at fishing by a girl. When she reeled in another snapper, I just couldn't take it anymore.

"How come you're catching all those fish, and Bobber and I can't even get a bite?" I asked.

"What's the porpoise in life?" she responded.

"The what?"

"The porpoise in life." she repeated. "What's the porpoise in life?"

"I dunno," I said. "Porpoise are mammals, and they breathe out of a blow hole, and they eat all kinds of fish. So, I guess it's to catch fish."

"Pretty close," she said. "The porpoise in life is not to flounder. You need to think about things from every angle so you can figure out the best way to do something. You guys aren't going to catch a fish until you hook your shrimp right. Think like the snapper for a change. You're killing your bait, and these snapper want live shrimp."

Coral then showed us how to hook a shrimp through the horn on the top of the head so it didn't kill the bait. For a girl, she sure knew a lot about fishing. Bobber and I quickly started getting bites, and in no time, we had five big snapper on the dock.

I was getting another shrimp out of the bait bucket when the entire dock started to shake.

"Earthquake! Tidal Wave! Tsunami!" yelled Bobber.

Coral and I held onto the pilings while the dock shook for about 10 seconds. Then the shaking stopped, and everything returned to normal . . . except for the fact that Coral's rope stringer and all the snapper she'd caught were gone.

Chapter 6

All Shook Up

Whatever it was that shook the dock, it sure scared us. Once the shaking stopped, Bobber kept saying, "See, there are alligators in the Keys. And they don't want us taking their snapper."

It took me a while to get Bobber to calm down. Coral was bummed because all her fish were gone, so I gave her two of the fish Bobber and I caught. After all, it was only fair. It was her dock we were fishing from, and we wouldn't have caught them without her help.

Bobber didn't want to give up the snapper. He said that we were obviously better at fishing than Coral because we had five fish and she had none, even though he knew she had caught more fish than both of us.

Coral wanted to keep fishing, but Bobber and I decided we'd had enough. We had to get back to the RV, or we'd miss the lobster dinner Uncle Pete was cooking.

Coral said she was going to clean the snapper, and her mom was going to cook them for dinner.

"Aren't you afraid of the dock monster?" asked Bobber as he backed away from the dock.

"Nah," said Coral. "It looks like it already ate its fill. It won't take long for me to clean these fish."

"If you want, I'll help," I offered, pulling out my pocket knife. "That way I can clean our fish, too."

Working together, it only took about ten minutes to clean the fish. Then Bobber and I walked back to the RV along a sandy path through the sea grape trees. On the driver's side of the Zephyr, Uncle Pete had built a pull-out stainless steel gas grill and fryer big enough to cook for the entire campground.

"Did you catch anything?" asked The Chief as we walked up to the RV where he and Uncle Pete were cooking lobster tails on the grill. We could smell their hard outer shells roasting. It smelled sweet, like summer corn roasting on the grill.

"Well, we did catch a mess of fish, but then some giant earthquake monster alligator ate them and almost pulled us into the water and ate us, too!" said Bobber excitedly.

"A what?" asked The Chief. "Slow down, Bobber."

"Don't listen to Bobber, Chief. He's still upset about being outfished by a girl," I said. "Something grabbed Coral's fish that were on a stringer and shook the whole dock."

"Wow, that could have been a big tarpon or possibly a shark," said Uncle Pete as he flipped a bright

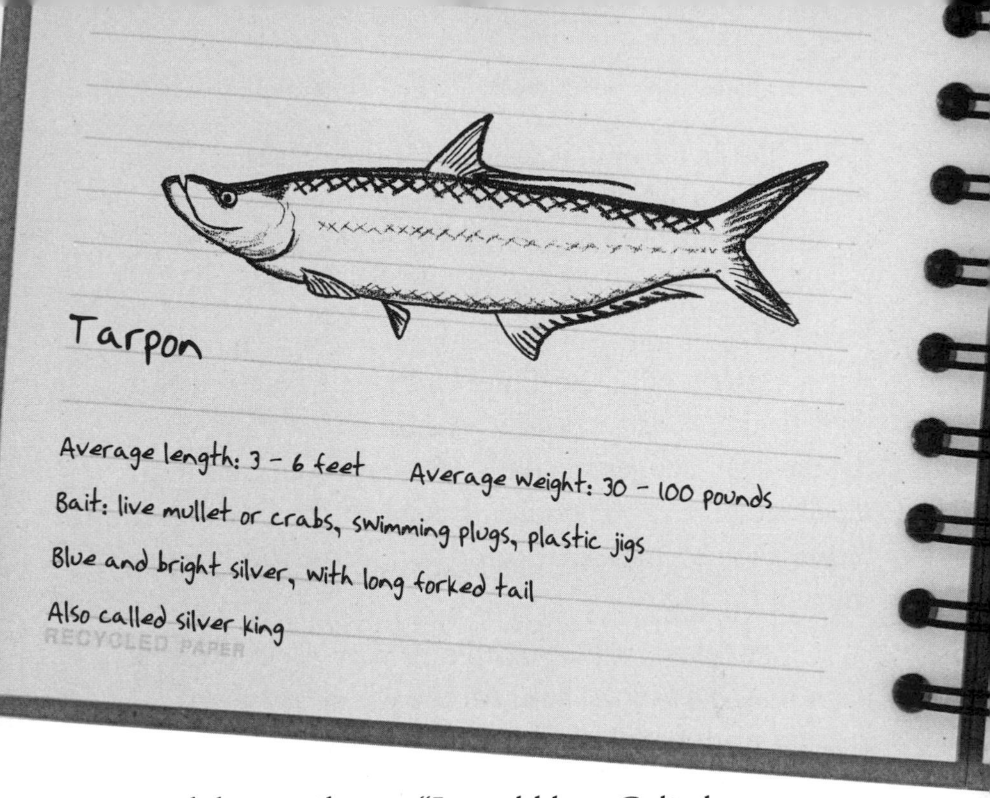

orange lobster tail over. "It could be a Goliath grouper, too. They grow to over 600 pounds."

"I still think it was an alligator," said Bobber.

"Whatever it was, it broke the stringer off the dock and stole all her fish. So Bobber and I gave her two of the fish we caught," I said.

"That's awful nice of you boys," said The Chief. "Maybe we should walk down there after dinner and see if we can figure out what it was."

"That'd be great, Chief," I replied.

"Oh, and just so you know, Bobber, I've been outfished by plenty of girls in my time. Boys, too," said The Chief. "It doesn't matter who you are or where you're from. Fishing is a skill that improves with knowledge and experience, and there's always someone with more of both."

Bobber and I ate lobster for the first time. I thought it tasted like chewy chicken, but because we ate the tails of the lobster and not the body, Bobber said it tasted more like chicken butt, which explains why it was so chewy.

Afterwards, The Chief and Uncle Pete grabbed their fishing rods and said it was time to walk down to the dock. It was getting dark, so we sprayed mosquito repellent all over our bodies. It kept the mosquitoes from biting us this time, but I could still hear them buzzing in front of my face.

The dock at Porpoise Point was black and aged from long days in the sun. All the wood had deep grooves from people walking on the planks. Some of the boards sagged from the heavy weight. There was a light on the end of the dock where it formed a "T."

The Chief said the light attracted shrimp and small baitfish, which made the larger fish come around to eat. We all walked out on the dock. Uncle Pete started casting his rod with a swimming plug on it.

On about the fifth or sixth cast, Uncle Pete got a tremendous bite, and his rod bent double as the line went screaming off.

I saw a huge silver flash out of the corner of my eye as the fish swam into the darkness. We could hear it jumping in the dark. It had to be huge!

Uncle Pete strained to hold onto his rod as the fish took all the line off his reel. In no time, he was out of line. With a loud *SNAP!*, the fish broke the knot at the end tied to the reel, and it was gone.

"That was crazy!" said Bobber. "That fish took all your line and never stopped. It must be the biggest fish in the ocean, maybe the world"

"I think that was a tarpon, boys," said Uncle Pete. "I forgot to bow to it, and it broke the line."

Bobber and I put one hand on our back and the other on our stomachs and started bowing over and over again. Uncle Pete and The Chief just laughed.

"Not bow, like you bow to a king or a pretty girl," said Uncle Pete. "Bow means to lean forward and thrust your rod forward to put slack into the line. You do that when the fish jumps so it doesn't pull the hook out or land on your line and break it."

"Okay," said Bobber. "Bow to the crazy-silver-jumping-tarpon fish. I can remember that."

As we were laughing at Bobber's joke, a pair of raccoons walked out from the shadows near the dock. They climbed a rope up onto one of the boats anchored in the marina. Inside the boat was a bait bucket. The raccoon used its paws to push open the lid on the plastic bucket, reach in, and then grab a shrimp. While the first raccoon was eating a shrimp, the second raccoon reached in and pulled out a pinfish.

"Holy masked mammals," said Bobber. "It's the bait bandits!"

"Well, at least we know what's happening to the bait in the buckets," said The Chief. "But what's grabbing the fish on the stringers?"

Chapter 7

Fishy Girl

In the morning, we saw Coral walking along the beach. She had her spinning rod, and she was towing a bait bucket behind her in the water. It was tied to a cord with one end of it wrapped around her waist. She had on a light blue long-sleeve shirt, shorts, sunglasses, and she was wearing funny-looking brown boots. Her straw hat was pulled down tight on her head like she was trying to hide under an umbrella. She also had a light blue bandana around her neck.

I ran up to her to tell her about the raccoons sneaking onto the boats in the marina and stealing people's bait and fish, but Bobber butted in.

"Hey Coral, what are you fishing for — fashion tips?" asked Bobber.

Coral did her saluting airplane take off wave. "I'm looking for bonefish, but you wouldn't know anything about them. They swim along the shore here at high tide. When they eat something off the bottom, their tails stick up in the air," said Coral as she scanned the water in front of her.

"Bonefish?" I said. "We read about them on the Internet. They swim into the current so they can smell their food. They mostly eat shrimp and crabs."

"That's right," said Coral. "And I'm going to cast a live shrimp at a school and catch one."

"Aw, I don't know if I want to eat a bonefish," said Bobber rubbing his belly. "I don't like bones in my fish, and it sounds like they have a lot of bones."

"You don't eat them, Bobber. You just catch them for fun and let them go. They're really fast, and when you hook them, they take almost all your line," noted Coral as she turned back to the water.

"Good thing you have us boys here to help you out, in case you actually do hook one. We can show you how to fight and land it in no time."

Coral rolled her eyes at Bobber's comment and then crouched down for a better look. The water on the

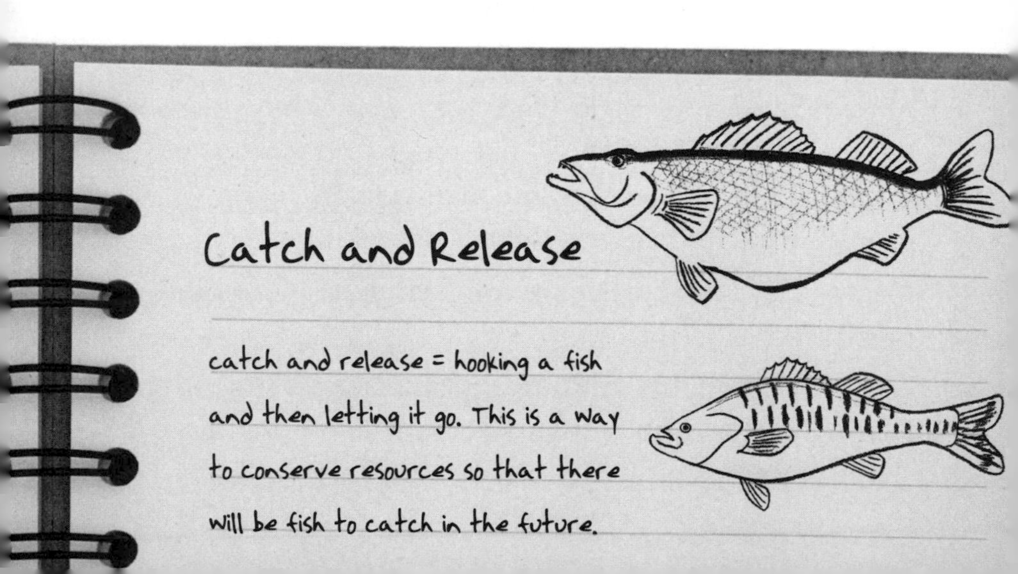

flats was crystal clear, giving it a light brown color over the grass and a turquoise color on the sand.

"There they are," whispered Coral, pointing to some rippling water about a foot deep and 50 feet from shore.

Five gray tails stuck out of the water and wiggled in the sunlight, throwing little drops of water off them. Just as quickly, they disappeared below the surface, but we could still see the ripples on the water as the fish moved ahead.

Coral put her finger to her lips to tell Bobber and me to keep quiet. Then she slowly took about ten steps forward. She cast her shrimp out ahead of the fish and waited for them to swim up. As the fish got closer, a tail popped out of the water and then everything exploded!

WHOOSH! went the school of fish as they swam full speed off the flat. *R-E-E-E-E-E!* screamed the reel as line went out.

"You've got a rocket! You've got a bullet! You've hooked a rocket-propelled, speeding bullet, creepy, boney skeleton fish!" said Bobber.

Coral calmly pulled back on the rod as the fish ran out 200 yards of line. It swam across the shallows and headed for deeper water. Just when it looked like she was going to run out of line, the fish stopped, and then Coral started pumping the rod up and down and reeling the fish back in.

"Whoa, check her out!" said Bobber with awe. For the first time, he couldn't hide the fact that he was impressed with Coral's fishing skills.

Bobber and I helped coach her — well, more like provided support — by saying things like, "You got it now," and, "Keep reeling, you're winning!" Coral fought the fish like an expert as it made two more runs, each one shorter than before.

As the fish came close to shore, we could see its silver sides and down-turned mouth. Just when it looked all tired out, it made a wide turn and bolted for the shallows.

"That's weird," said Coral. "That fish should be done." Then she paused and her eyes got wide as she said, "Oh no, a barracuda!"

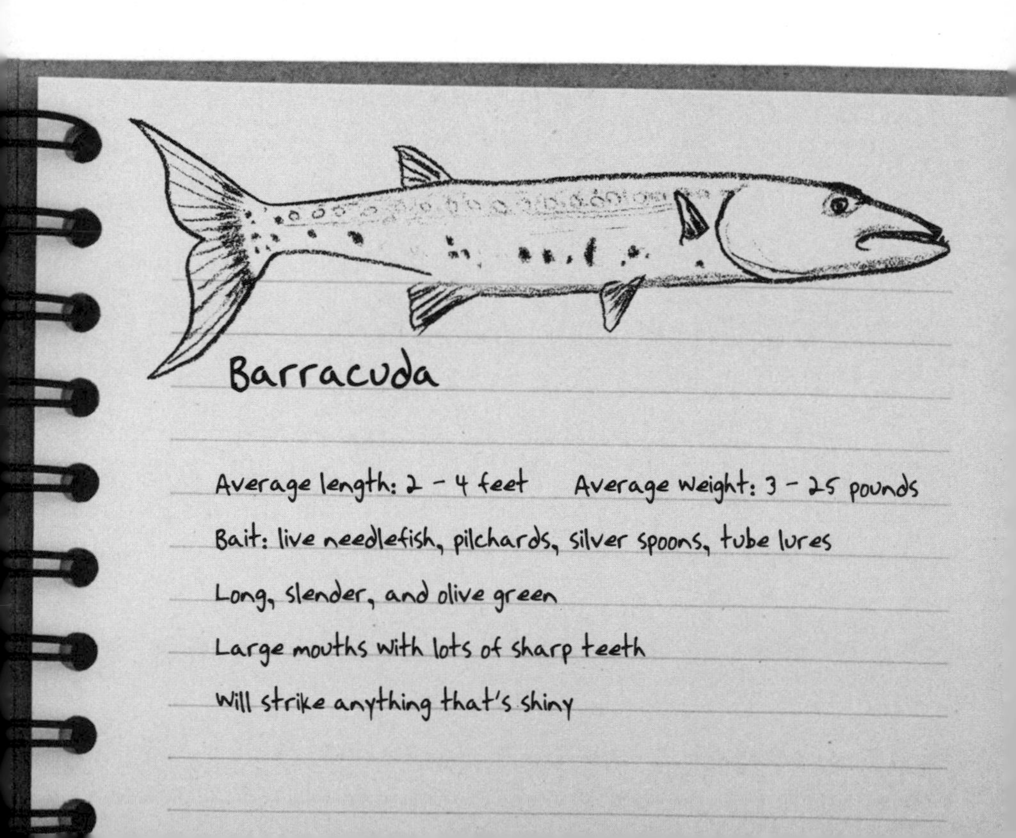

Chapter 8

Cuda Town

"A barracuda!" I yelled as I ran for shore.

"A barracuda!" Bobber yelled as he ran for shore.

"A barracuda!" Coral yelled as she ran out into the water, waving her hands and slapping her fishing rod on the surface.

Bobber and I looked at each other in disbelief. What was she doing?

"Get away from my bonefish you snaggle-toothed poacher!" Coral exclaimed. She was running straight *towards* the barracuda.

The four-foot long fish was shaped like an arrow and had teeth like a steel trap. With a kick of its tail, it rushed across the flat and caught the tired bonefish between its teeth. Coral kept running at the barracuda and slapping her fishing rod on the surface, but it was no use. The barracuda bit through her monofilament fishing line, and with the bonefish in its jaws, it swam slowly off into deeper water.

Coral hung her head.

"Did you see that?" I said. "That was amazing. That barracuda caught your bonefish and ate it. I would have thought there wasn't a fish in the ocean that could catch a bonefish."

"I know," said Coral. "It's all my fault."

"Huh? You didn't do anything," I said.

"The only reason that barracuda caught that bonefish was because it was tired out. I fought it too long. That gave the barracuda a chance to catch it. It's my fault," said Coral.

"Are you kidding? I'd pay cash money to see that again!" exclaimed Bobber. "That was the coolest thing I've ever seen. I wish I could catch one. See if you can hook another one and get the barracuda to eat it, too," he pleaded.

"No, I'm done for the morning. I don't want to catch any more bonefish," said Coral as she started walking back to her house.

Bobber and I walked back up to the RV where Uncle Pete and The Chief were getting their fishing gear ready. We were going to fish outside the reef today for mahi and wahoo and tuna. On the walk, Bobber was still wondering why Coral went home.

"Coral didn't seem to want to fish anymore," said Bobber. "Even after that supersonic barracuda missile ate that bonefish in one gulp."

"She didn't want to fish anymore because she was afraid the barracuda would eat another bonefish. She likes to catch the bonefish for fun. Letting the barracuda eat them is not part of the fun, Bobber," I explained.

"But it was cool. That barracuda just came in and whoosh! It snatched the bonefish out of the water," he said.

"You don't understand, Bobber. If you keep catching bonefish, then the barracuda will eat them all, and you won't have any more bonefish to catch for fun," I said. "If they always get eaten, then they won't come here anymore."

"Oh, I never thought of it like that," said Bobber. "I thought that bonefish was super cool, too, and I wouldn't want her to ruin the fishing forever. I guess that's why they catch them and let them go, so there will always be bonefish to catch around here."

As we approached the RV and Uncle Pete and The Chief, Bobber leaned over and elbowed me in the side and said, "I'll bet it was a giant barracuda that ate the snapper on the stringer last night."

WATER
ZEPHYR

Chapter 9

Blue Water Cowboys

"Wow, those rods and reels look pretty heavy duty," I said to Uncle Pete as he loaded the gear into the boat. "Are we fishing for whales?"

Uncle Pete lifted out a big trolling rod and explained what he had planned for the day.

"We need these conventional reels because they hold more line than a spinning reel. If we hook a big mahi or a wahoo, or even a marlin, we don't want to be running out of line. We can even lock the drag down, and let it pull the boat around like a sled dog."

"How big do mahi get?" asked Bobber.

"They can be 60 pounds or more. Wahoo can get over 100 pounds, and marlin can be 400 pounds. They're big fish, guys," said Uncle Pete. "This is the Atlantic Ocean, and at one time or another, anything under 100 pounds can be considered bait."

Average length: 30 - 40 inches Average weight: 20 - 50 pounds

Bait: rigged ballyhoo with red and black skirt, live bait with wire leader

Long body with tiny scales

Bright blue back and silvery sides with blue bar patterns

Can swim 50 miles per hour!

RECYCLED PAPER

I helped Uncle Pete load the rods and reels and the cooler while Bobber and The Chief grabbed drinks and sandwiches for everyone. We were going to spend the entire day on the water, and we didn't want to get hungry or thirsty and have to come in. That would spoil our fishing.

In no time, we had the boat loaded and everyone was on board as we headed out towards Alligator Lighthouse. Uncle Pete had a baseball cap pulled down on his head and was wearing his pilot's goggles as he pushed the throttle forward. The *Water Zephyr* jumped up onto the waves.

"Wa-hoo!" yelled Uncle Pete as the boat motored across the flat, calm, dark blue ocean.

"The Gulf Stream flows from the West Coast of Florida, around the tip of the Keys, and then north up the East Coast," said Uncle Pete. "We're going to head

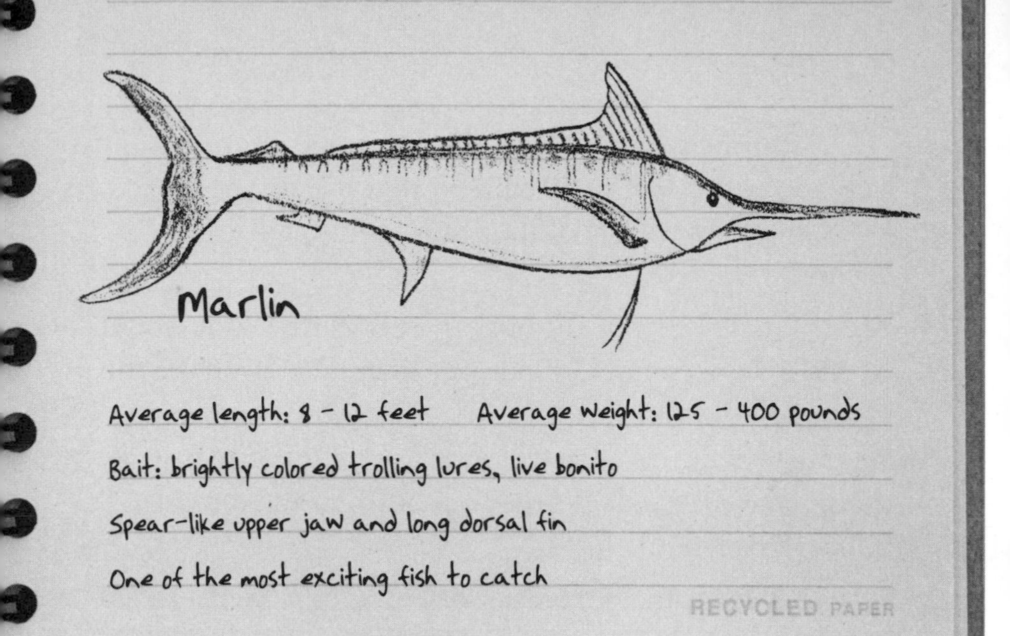

southeast and then troll our way back north. That will put us off Islamorada by the end of the day."

As we passed Alligator Light, I saw the reef where we had gone diving for lobsters the day before. At first, the water was clear and milky green colored, and then it started to turn a dark navy blue, and then bright, vibrant royal blue.

"That's the color change," said Uncle Pete. "Every time we drop off to deeper water, it gets clearer and cleaner, and you can see a different shade of blue. This color change is about four miles from land."

I got out my FishingKids compass and watched the needle point southeast. Islamorada got smaller on the horizon. The Atlantic Ocean was a lot bigger than White Bear Lake, and I was afraid we were going to be out of sight of land when Uncle Pete stopped the boat.

"Lines in, boys," said Uncle Pete.

On the way out, The Chief had rigged some ballyhoo, which are small baitfish that live on the reef. The Chief says it's one of the main food items for offshore gamefish.

Uncle Pete put the boat in gear as slow as it would go while Bobber and I let out our lines. We could see the rigged ballyhoo at the end of the lines swimming along like they were alive. The Chief had put a green plastic thing that looked like a tiny mop head on the top of Bobber's ballyhoo.

"Why is that green bag on my lure, Chief?" asked Bobber.

"That's called a skirt, and we put it over the bait to add more color so fish can see if from a long ways away," said The Chief.

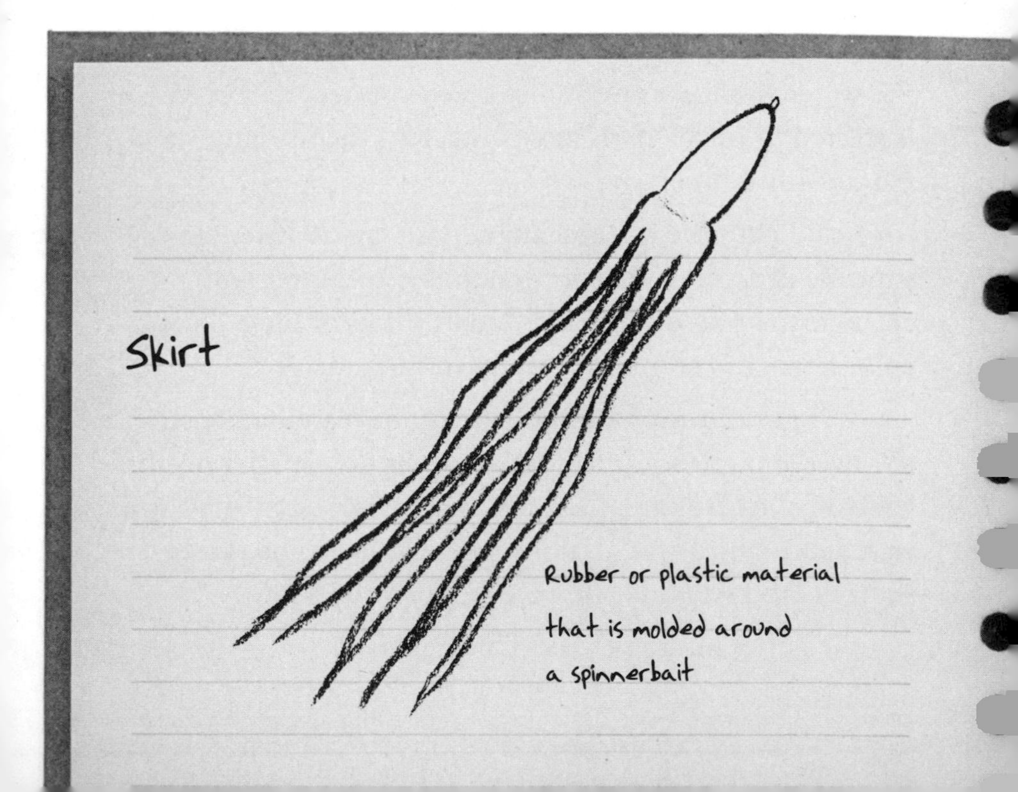

"A skirt?" said Bobber. "How do you know my ballyhoo is a girl? What if it's a boy ballyhoo, and you're making it wear a skirt? All the other ballyhoo will make fun of it."

Bobber then held a skirt over the tail half of a ballyhoo and shook it to make the ballyhoo look like it was dancing. Everyone laughed at the plastic attractor on the baitfish, and Uncle Pete did a hula dance. We were all lying back in the boat laughing and trying to catch our breath when Bobber's rod bent over, and a fish jumped out of the water.

"Leaping yellow jackets!" said Bobber as he set the hook hard, hitting himself in the head with the rod and knocking his hat off. "It's a giant swarm of jumping dolphinfish!"

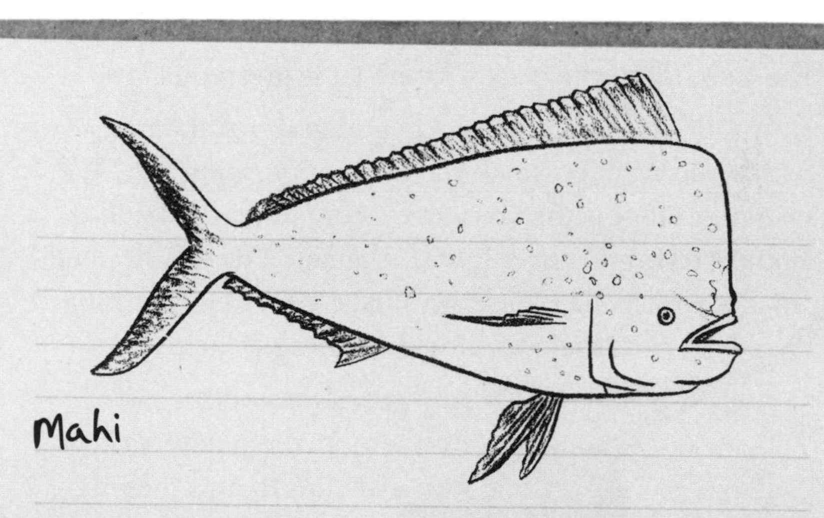

Average length: 2 - 4 feet   Average weight: 10 - 30 pounds

Bait: rigged ballyhoo with green or pink skirt, yellow feather jig

Bright gold, blue, and green

Also called dolphinfish

The bright blue and green fish were easy to see through the clear blue water as 30 or more mahi followed Bobber's hooked fish to the back of the boat.

Bobber's mahi was about four feet long with a forked tail and a large, blunt head. The fish jumped from the water several times, and it was so strong that The Chief had to help Bobber hold onto the rod. With some extra help from The Chief, he reeled the fish to the side of the boat where Uncle Pete grabbed the line and pulled it into the boat with a loud *FLOP!*

FLOP, FLOP, THUNKA, THUNKA, FLOP went the fish as it hit the deck, kicking and jumping and bouncing all around, with the hook sticking out of its mouth and its tail swinging wildly.

"It's after me!" yelled Bobber as he scrambled to get away from the crazy bouncing mahi.

"Get it, Bobber," I said as I chased the flopping fish around on the deck. "Don't let it jump out."

Bobber reacted quickly and grabbed the net, which was way too small for the big, flopping fish. We chased it around the boat, me trying to grab its tail, Bobber trying to cover it with the net. The fish flopped madly while The Chief and Uncle Pete were laughing so hard they couldn't do a thing to help.

I finally got a hold on the tail, Bobber put the net over the fish's head, and then we both jumped on top of the flopping mahi. The fish flopped several more times,

and every time it flopped, it would bounce Bobber and me into the air like we were riding a bucking bull. Eventually, the flopping stopped.

The Chief and Uncle Pete were still laughing hysterically when The Chief finally caught his breath. He pointed to our shirts and said, "Great job, boys. As much as you love fishing, I've always known you guys had scales."

We looked down and both of us were covered in fish slime and fish scales. It was all over our shirts, pants, shoes, and even our arms and legs.

"Just don't fall overboard, or something that eats mahi might have you for dinner," said Uncle Pete as he pulled down his pilot's goggles, started the boat, and then put it in gear at trolling speed. "Now let's see if we can catch some more mahi, or even a wahoo!"

Chapter 10

The Dock Monster

By the time we got in from mahi fishing, we were all tuckered out from reeling in fish and chasing them around the boat until they calmed down.

Instead of anchoring on the beach and wading to shore, Uncle Pete steered the boat to Porpoise Point Marina, where Coral was waiting to help us tie up to the dock. Bobber and I offered to help clean the fish. We got them out of the cooler and brought them to the fish cleaning table at the end of the dock.

We had ten big mahi and a single small blackfin tuna. The Chief showed me how to clean a mahi, and then a tuna. We all cleaned fish with The Chief doing most of the hard work. When we were done, there were three big bags of fillets, and The Chief gave one to Coral for letting us use her fish cleaning table.

"Thank you, Chief," said Coral. "And you guys can throw all the carcasses in the water. That should get the big snapper all chummed up."

Coral was right. In no time, there were big fish eating what was left of the mahi we caught. First snapper came in and picked at the meat. Then big jack crevalles, which have a round head like a pumpkin.

"Hey look, it's Sally," said Coral as she pointed to a large dark object rising off the bottom.

We all looked down into the water where a big yellow shark was pushing against the dock as it munched on a piece of mahi.

Bobber immediately jumped off the dock and onto land.

"It's the dock monster! Chief, Uncle Pete, it's the man-eating, dock-shaking, monster shark of Porpoise Point!" he hollered.

The Chief and Uncle Pete immediately walked over to the dock.

"That's a nurse shark," said Uncle Pete. "They're pretty docile as sharks go. They're not man-eaters."

"Oh yeah?" replied Bobber. "Why would they call them nurse sharks if they can't put you in the hospital?"

"They've got small teeth, and they live under the ledges of the reef," said Uncle Pete. "You boys don't have to worry. That shark isn't going to eat you. Although, she could bite you pretty good if you tried to grab her."

"See? And it's big enough that it could pull the whole dock off the seawall," said Bobber as he leaned over the side for a better look at the massive shark.

The cement seawall at Porpoise Point Marina was full of big cracks and holes from being battered by storms, and there was an area that had collapsed and left a big hole that went under the water. Along the water's edge were sharp-edged oysters and barnacles and other marine shells stuck to the cement.

"Well, it's about 10 feet long, so it's pretty powerful. It probably could shake the dock if it grabbed a stringer tied to the pilings," said Uncle Pete.

Coral seemed amused by Bobber's ramblings. "I told you, Bobber, that's just Sally," said Coral. "That shark comes here all the time. She's no monster."

"See, see?" Bobber continued. "It's got girl Cootie nurse teeth for shaking people off the pilings so it can eat them. It even has a girly name, Sally."

"You sure are funny," said Coral. "But looks aren't everything. Would you feel better if I called it Fred?"

Just as if the nurse shark heard the conversation, it left, leaving the tarpon, snapper, and even a small barracuda to eat the rest of the scraps.

"Well, if it wasn't a shark, and it wasn't an alligator, then what's been stealing all the fish off the stringer and shaking the dock?" asked Bobber.

Chapter 11

Snapper Champs

Coral invited Bobber and me back to her dock to fish for snapper after dinner. We were so excited, we gobbled our food down quickly, and The Chief said we were like human garbage disposals.

We met Coral at the dock about an hour before the sun went down. When we got there, she had a cardboard sign stapled to the dock that read "Islamorada Snapper Champion — Any Dock. Anywhere. Anytime."

Bobber and I just laughed.

"You may think it's funny," said Coral. "But I can outfish anyone when it comes to catching snapper."

I said that she sure beat us the other day, but once we learned how to hook the shrimp so they wouldn't die, we had caught just as many fish as she had.

Coral ran the braided cord of hair through her fingers and spun the lure on the end in little circles.

"You guys may know how to catch muskies, but no one knows how to catch snapper better than me," said Coral with a hint of pride in her voice. "I've won the Islamorada Kids Fishing Tournament three times. I even beat some of the kids whose dads are fishing guides."

"I bet Spinner or I could beat you," boasted Bobber, waving his hands excitedly at the thought of being the Snapper Champ of Islamorada. "How about we have a tournament right now?"

"You're on," said Coral. "Grab your shrimp buckets and let's head out to the dock."

At that point, I wasn't sure what Bobber had gotten us into. Coral was really good at fishing. She'd even caught bonefish and tarpon before. I thought about backing out, but Bobber gave me a shove and whispered, "We've got a secret weapon, my lucky Shoe Bait."

Bobber winked at me and tilted his head towards the special lure he keeps hooked into his shoe. When we were fishing in Minnesota last summer, Bobber got a lure caught on one of his Crocs, and he decided to keep it there for good luck.

The fishing that day was really fun. Every time one of us cast, in a few minutes a snapper would grab our bait. Sometimes we hooked and landed the fish, and sometimes they swiped our baits, and we had to put another shrimp on the hook.

I was getting the hook out of a snapper, when it clamped down and wouldn't let go.

"That's why they call them snapper," said Coral. "They'll chomp down on your finger if you let them.

And with those big fangs for teeth, you'll remember it forever."

After about an hour, Coral was in the lead with five snapper. Bobber had three snapper and I had two, when Bobber took off his shoe and pulled the Shoe Bait off his Croc.

He held it up and showed it to Coral. "This is my top-secret, super-duper, never-let-me-down, gonna-make-the-fish-frown lucky Shoe Bait. And it's going to catch everything in this marina," said Bobber as he tied the lure on his hook.

He made a cast, let the Shoe Bait settle, and then started jigging the rod as he reeled the lure back in. The snapper followed it. Coral looked on skeptically.

On the next cast, he reeled slower and got a bite.

"I got one!" yelled Bobber, jerking back on the rod and knocking his hat off in the process. "I'm the Shoe Bait-iest snapper trapper on Islamorada!"

That gave him four snapper. But Coral still had five on her stringer.

On the next cast, he caught another one.

"Zingo! It's snapper time!" said an elated Bobber as he added a fifth snapper to his stringer.

Bobber made another cast, and another snapper struck his lucky Shoe Bait. As he was reeling the fish in, a large dark object swam slowly out from under the dock.

"Holy four-wheeler, it's a swimming truck!" said Bobber, as the massive fish came out into the open.

The fish was giant, and it seemed like it took forever for its entire body to come out from under the dock. It swam slowly towards Bobber's snapper, and when it got about a foot away, it opened its huge mouth and sucked the little snapper in.

"Oh my, that's a Goliath grouper," said Coral breathlessly as she watched the fish slowly meander back underneath the dock. "They're protected. You can't keep them."

The Goliath grouper was the size of all three of us put together. It was a mustard-yellow color with big

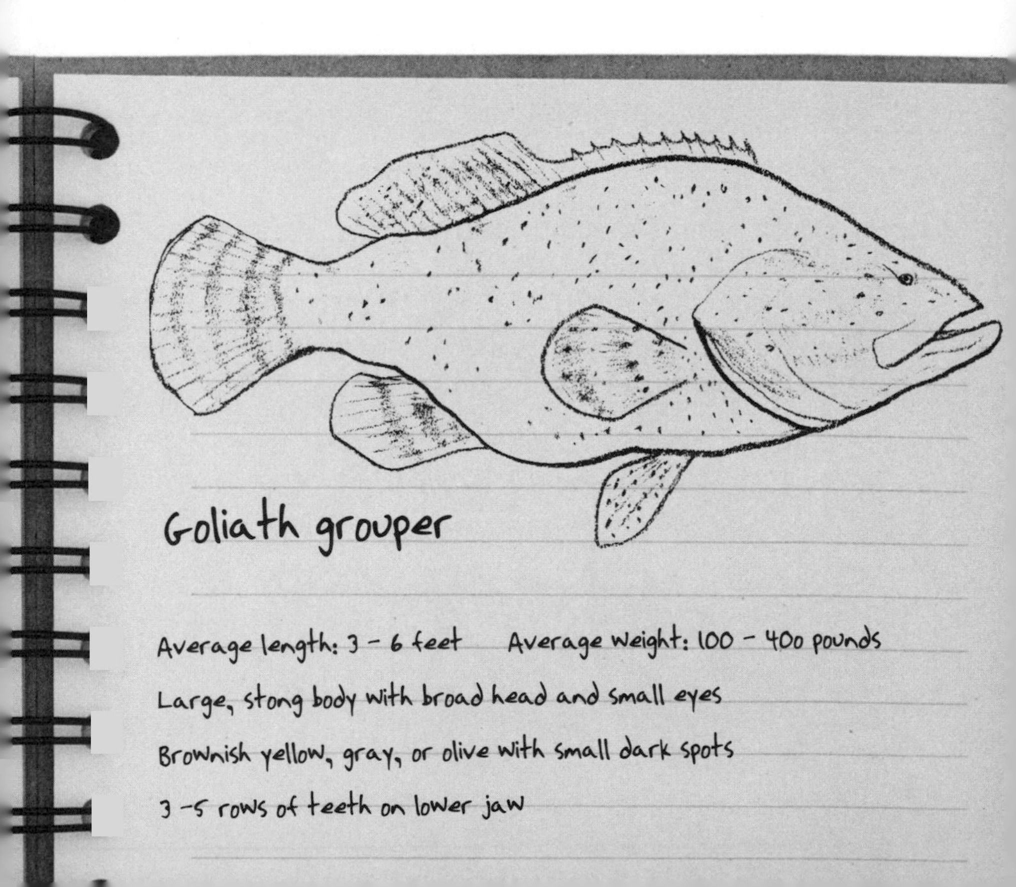

splotches all over its body like someone had thrown brown paint against its side. The fish had a giant mouth that it kept opening and closing, small round eyes, and a wide swooping tail that allowed it to move forward with gentle little kicks.

Bobber and I were just staring, amazed at the size of the huge fish when Bobber realized he was now hooked to the Goliath grouper. His eyes got large, his rod bent double, and it almost pulled him off the dock.

"It's the Shoe Bait! It's my lucky Shoe Bait! It's the best snapper-Goliath-grouper-catching bait in the whole wide ocean!" exclaimed Bobber as he strained to hang on to his fishing rod.

The Goliath grouper acted like it didn't even know it was hooked. It swam back under the dock, taking Bobber's snapper, Shoe Bait, and line with it. Finally, the line broke. and Bobber fell over backwards, off the dock and the grass.

"I had him, Spinner. I had the Goliath of Porpoise Point. I almost caught the biggest snapper-eating fish on Islamorada," said Bobber.

Chapter 12

Grouper Trooper

Bobber was still lying on his back when the Goliath grouper came back out from under the dock, and with one big bite, sucked all the fish on Coral's stringer into its mouth. The grouper then started to pull and shake.

"It's shaking the dock," said Coral as she stepped back onto the grass next to Bobber. "Hurry up, Spinner, it's going to pull the dock into the water."

I don't know why, but I just had a feeling that fish wasn't going to pull the dock into the water. The fish probably weighed 400 pounds, and was about six feet long, but it didn't swim very fast. It just kind of shook its head as it tried to break the stringer loose from the piling.

"It's going to shake you off the dock and eat you like a snapper-headed snack!" said Bobber.

"No guys, it's just trying to pull the snapper off the stringer. It's looking for a meal," I said, as I leaned over, grabbed the stringer, and pulled back.

For a few seconds, the Goliath grouper and I were in a big tug-o-war. Then the stringer broke, and I fell backwards onto the dock. Coral and Bobber laughed and said I was lucky I didn't get pulled into the water.

The Goliath grouper sat motionless next to the pilings as Bobber, Coral, and I looked down at the giant fish. Then with a kick of its mighty tail, it moved slowly forward.

"He's going for my fish!" yelled Bobber as he ran down the dock to where his stringer of snapper was hanging in the water. "You're not going to eat my catch, you bug-eyed garbage can!"

Bobber and the Goliath grouper reached the stringer at the same time. Bobber pulled on one end while the Goliath grouper pulled on the other. Coral and I ran over and helped Bobber pull back on the stringer.

We pulled so hard, the Goliath grouper's entire head came out of the water. Then it let go of the stringer, and we pulled the fish up onto the dock.

"I'm the Snapper King of the World!" hollered Bobber, and he held up the snapper he had caught. "Not even the giant Goliath grouper can catch snapper better than me."

Coral had to admit that Bobber did catch more snapper, but only because the Goliath grouper ate hers. I told Bobber he was the snappiest snapper snagger I knew. We could see the Goliath grouper sitting under the dock where there was a hole in the seawall. Now we knew where its home was.

The Goliath grouper was under water on its side, right next to the pilings, as Bobber, Coral, and I looked down at the fish. It was then that we realized something was wrong. Instead of moving slowly along, the gentle giant was leaning to one side and struggling to swim straight.

As we watched, we could see that the grouper was having a hard time swimming because a long white cord was wrapped around its back and belly. The cord was so tight, it looked like it was digging into the fish's skin, and it had one of its side fins pinned against its body.

"No wonder it's eating all our fish. It has a lobster line wrapped around its body and can hardly swim," said Coral with sadness in her voice. "It can't fish for itself. It's starving to death."

"It looks like his side is scratched up, too," said Bobber. "He looks really sad and tired. We need to do something to help him."

"What can we do?" said Coral. "He's too big to get in the water with. He might hurt us."

"I'll bet The Chief and Uncle Pete will know what to do," I said. "They're always getting us out of messes back home. Maybe if they can get the line off its body, it'll be able to go catch its own food and stop eating fish off of people's stringers."

We quickly ran to the Zephyr and told Uncle Pete and The Chief about the injured fish. Uncle Pete used the satellite phone to call the Ranger Station and the Florida Marine Patrol, who sent over a fish biologist. The biologist had a heavy rope fishing line with a big circle hook on one the end. As he got ready to catch the Goliath grouper, the entire campground gathered around to watch.

"I need something to tie this line off to," said the biologist. "It might pull the boards off if I tie it to the dock."

"I've got just the thing. Be back in a minute," said Uncle Pete as he ran off down the trail.

The biologist put a chunk of fish on the end of the hook, and he was talking to Coral's dad when we heard a loud air horn. *WHONK!* went the horn from the Zephyr as Uncle Pete drove around the corner and up to the marina wall.

He backed the Zephyr up to the wall, and with a loud *WHOOSH!*, the RV came to a stop. Uncle Pete leaned out the driver's side window, pilot's goggles on his head, and said, "Tie the line to the trailer hitch. There's no way that fish can out-pull the Zephyr."

The biologist tied the line to the trailer hitch and then pitched the bait into the water right in front of the Goliath grouper. The fish ate the chunk of fish, hook and all, and when it tried to swim away, the line came tight.

Coral's dad and the biologist held onto the line while directing Uncle Pete to inch the Zephyr forward. Uncle Pete watched all the action through the rear-facing camera in the Zephyr. When the fish surfaced, it was tired and all out of fight.

That's when Coral's dad and the biologist jumped into the water and started cutting the line off the Goliath grouper. The line had wrapped around the fish's tail and then its back and mid-section, and every time the fish tried to swim, it had cut into its back. The line had made about a four inch deep cut into the fish, and the biologist had to pull the line out slowly by cutting it into little pieces.

When the rope came loose, everyone cheered. Uncle Pete let out a blast with the air horn, *WHONK!*, and Bobber, Coral, and I all high-fived each other. The biologist also took three big hooks and one small lure out of the Goliath grouper's mouth.

"That's my lucky Shoe Bait!" said Bobber when the biologist put the lure up on the dock.

The biologist decided to leave the Goliath grouper in the water instead of taking it to the marine animal hospital. He said it would take three or four weeks for the wounds to heal. Then it might move on.

Coral, Bobber, and I made fliers that we posted around the Islamorada Campgrounds explaining what had happened and asking all anglers to come down to the Porpoise Point Marina to clean their fish and to throw the scraps to the Goliath grouper at the dock.

Chapter 13

FishingKids

For the next few days, Bobber, Coral, and I would spend the afternoons catching snapper. Now, instead of putting our catch on stringers that dangled in the water, we put them in a bucket next to where we were fishing. When we were done fishing, we'd clean our fish on the cleaning table at the end of the dock. As soon as we ran the hose to clean off the table, the Goliath grouper would come out from under the dock so we could feed it. Coral named the Goliath grouper "Conchy," which she said is a nickname for the locals who live in the Keys.

"It's like a pet fish," said Bobber as he threw a piece of a snapper into the water. "You've got the coolest giant monster bug-eyed garbage can fish on Islamorada!"

"That hose is like a fish call," I said, tossing some snapper parts into the water where Conchy quickly gobbled them down. "Every time you run the hose, Conchy knows it's dinner time."

"You sure have the coolest pet I've ever seen, Coral," I said as I watched the Goliath grouper swallow fish parts whole. "Not everyone has their own swimming vacuum cleaner."

"It is pretty neat. My dad says the fliers we made have all the campers using the fish cleaning table. Now, Conchy has an endless supply of food," said Coral. "Yesterday, he had his back out of the water under the dock, so I leaned over and rubbed it, and all his fins stuck out like he really liked it."

"Totally cool," said Bobber with awe.

Just then, Coral's dad walked up. He had a surprise for us.

"Because the three of you went beyond what's expected to take care of our natural resources, the Islamorada Campgrounds want to make you lifetime Park Scouts," said Coral's dad as he handed us ID cards with our names on them. "You can stay here for free any time you're in Islamorada."

We all smiled and thanked him. Bobber reached down, pulled the lure off his Croc, and turned to Coral.

"I want you to have my lucky Shoe Bait," said Bobber. "It makes you a real FishingKid, and besides, you're the Snapper Queen of Islamorada. I really didn't think girls can fish, but you proved me wrong."

I was happy that Bobber finally admitted to Coral how impressed he was by her. I said to Coral, "Bobber can be hard-headed sometimes, but he's my best friend for a reason. He had to figure you out for himself, but I knew he'd come around." I had a feeling that Bobber, Coral, and I would be friends for life.

Coral got to give Bobber's Shoe Bait a try. The three of us spent the day fishing for bonefish and tarpon while Uncle Pete and The Chief got the *Water Zephyr* loaded back on the trailer and packed the RV. It was going to be a long ride back to White Bear Lake, Minnesota.

We waded in the flats in front of the campground looking for schooling bonefish. We walked around the itch mud, casting live shrimp in front of any tails we saw sticking up. Bobber caught a box fish, which looks kind of like a tiny square cow. It has horns and everything.

At one point, Bobber had a bite from a bonefish that went racing across the flat and almost pulled the rod out of his hands. When he set the hook, he did it so hard he knocked the hat off his head with his fishing rod, again. The hat landed in the water, the fish took a bunch of line, and then spit out the hook.

"That was crazy racing rocket ship fast," said Bobber. "The next time we come to the Keys, I'm going to work on being the Bonefish Catching Champion of the World."

Coral just smiled at Bobber and said, "First you have to catch one. Right now, you're the Bonefish Losing Champion of the World."

We all laughed as Bobber put his wet hat back on his head.

Uncle Pete honked the air horn on the RV, and we all waded to shore. When we walked up to the Zephyr, we saw a small map of Florida hand-painted on the driver side just below the window. Across the state was painted a lobster, a tarpon, and a Goliath grouper.

“What is that map on the side for Uncle Pete?” I asked, pointing to the still wet paint.

“That’s my mission log,” said Uncle Pete. “When I was a pilot, we would paint little insignias on our airplanes after every dangerous mission. Now, I’m going to paint one on the Zephyr after every great fishing trip.”

The Florida mission sure had been a great success. As we said goodbye to Coral, she pulled my FishingKids Notebook out of my hand, opened it to a blank page, and drew a picture of a girl with a fishing rod. Then she wrote her e-mail address below it so we could keep in touch, and she could tell us how Conchy was doing. I wasn’t surprised when I saw that her e-mail address contained the name “fishygirl.”

Bobber and I boarded the Zephyr, climbed up into the bubble canopy seats, opened the lids, and put on our pilot's goggles. Uncle Pete let off the air breaks, and the Zephyr let out an audible *WHOOSH!* as he shouted, "Wa-hoo!"

In no time, we pulled out onto A1A, the main road that runs through the Florida Keys. I took out my FishingKids compass, got a bearing, and pointed.

"North by Northwest, Uncle Pete," I said. "We're heading home."

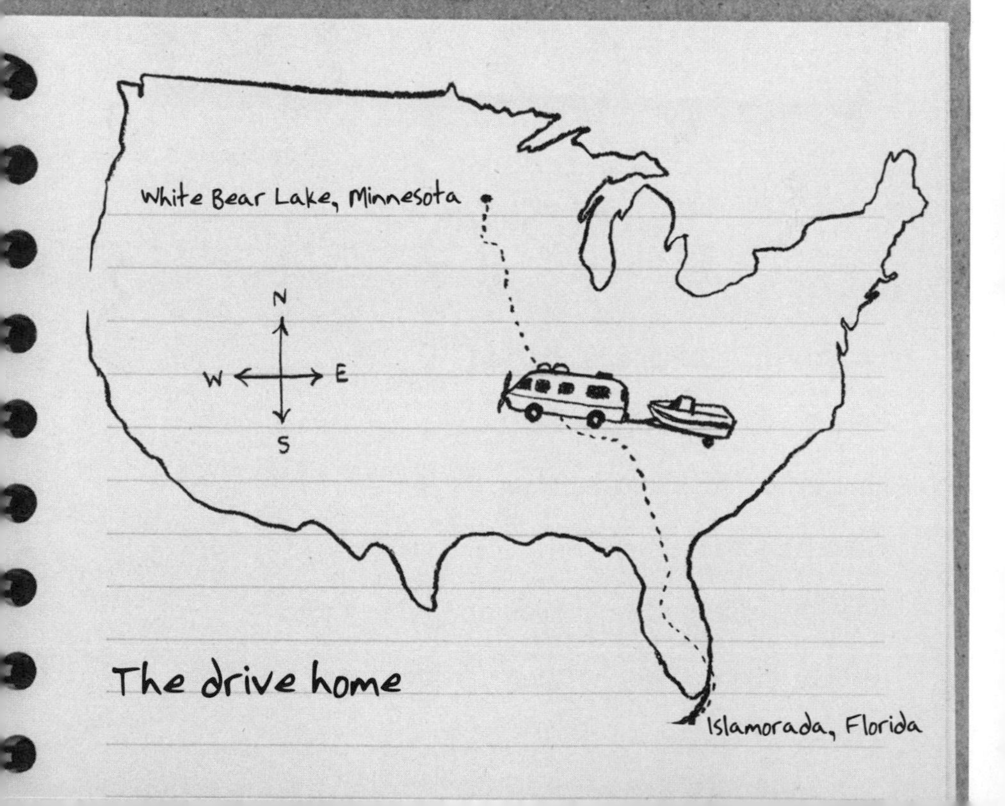

Coral Skye

Age: 11

Hometown: Islamorada, Florida

Hobbies: fishing and snorkeling

Largest catch: 45 pound Mahi

Favorite foods: fresh fruit, fresh vegetables, fresh fish

Special skills: baiting a hook and tying knots

Always wears: straw hat and a fishing lure and beads woven into hair

Coral is one-of-a-kind. She's a spunky, independent, outdoorsy girl who knows all the best fishing spots from trips with her dad. She's tough, smart, compassionate, creative, and has a never-give-up attitude.

She has Native American ancestry. Her father's family is part Seminole.

Her favorite subject in school is science, and she wants to be a pilot and/or an astronaut someday.

Coral is also very creative. Once she made jewelry out of fishing lures for all of her friends.

Steven Pinner (or Spinner)

Age: 10

Hometown: White Bear Lake, Minnesota

Hobbies: fishing, sketching, more fishing, biking, and fishing

Largest catch: 30 pound muskie on White Bear Lake

Favorite foods: hot dogs and baked beans

Special skills: cleaning fish and reading maps

Always wears: his fishing vest

Bobby Ernest (or Bobber)

Age: 10

Hometown: White Bear Lake, Minnesota

Hobbies: fishing, more fishing, camping, and pulling pranks

Largest catch: Goliath Grouper (by accident!)

Favorite food: homemade mac n cheese

Special skills: findig worms and telling jokes

Always wears: his red and white T-shirt

The Chief

Age: ? (that's not polite to ask of old timers)

Hometown: White Bear Lake, Minnesota

Job: Structural Engineer (retired)

Hobbies: fishing, reading the newspaper, and putting back together anything that is broken

Biggest fish caught: 210 pound Halibut

Favorite food: Grandma Pinner's lasagna

Uncle Pete

Age: 50

Hometown: Lakeville, Minnesota

Job: Pilot (recently retired)

Hobbies: fishing, tinkering with the Zephyr, planning fishing trips, camping, and (once in while) golf

Biggest fish caught: 180 pound Marlin

Favorite food: BBQ ribs with corn on the cob

If you enjoyed that last story, check out my next fishing advnture. Bobber and I are heading down to Louisiana with The Chief and Uncle Pete. Here's a sneak peak.
The Pirate of Creole Bay

Prologue

Bobber and I were walking up from the dock when we saw the garage door was open at The Chief's house. Uncle Pete's RV was parked out front.

"Looks like your grandfather is planning another fishing trip," said Bobber. "Your Uncle Pete doesn't bring the Zephyr over unless they're going somewhere."

When we got to the garage, The Chief was sitting at his work bench. He had a spinning reel taken apart and was using a tube to put grease on the gears inside the reel. Uncle Pete was nowhere in sight.

"Hey, Chief!" I said. "What'cha doing?"

"Just working on one of my fishing reels. Got to keep them in good shape if I want them to catch fish," said The Chief.

"We just caught some fish down on the dock," said Bobber. " I got a two pound smallmouth!"

"That's a nice fish for a warm summer morning," said The Chief matter-of-factly as he went back to working on the reel.

"Yeah, but nothing like the fish we catch when we go on a trip with you and Uncle Pete," said Bobber, hinting at the possibility of a new fishing adventure.

"We always have fun on our trips, Chief," I followed. "Wish we could go on another one someday."

The Chief didn't even look up. Instead, he just nodded his head, put the tube of grease down, and started putting the reel back together.

We stood there for awhile waiting for The Chief to say more, and it was really silent for a long time. I started to feel kind of weird and uncomfortable, when all of a sudden the door leading into the house burst open and out stepped Uncle Pete. At least, I think it was Uncle Pete.

He had on blue jean overalls with the legs tucked into a pair of white rubber boots, a camouflage sweatshirt, and the head of an alligator with its mouth open pulled down over his face.

"Who dat' be wantin' to go a-fishin'?" he said, with an accent I could barely understand. "We got us some bandy crawfish heah!"

"Great gator goggles," giggled Bobber. "It's the swamp-faced fisherman!"

"Nah, it's only Uncle Pete," I said, moving closer so I could lift up the nose of the gator and see his face. "Why are you dressed up like an alligator trapper?"

"Because we're heading for the Louisiana marshes. Sportsman's Paradise! Where the bass and redfish swim together with the alligators, and there's more water than land," he replied. "I hope you boys like boiled crawfish and blackened redfish because we're going to have us a regular Cajun fishing trip!"

Bobber and I were both over the moon, and after hearing the details of the trip, I rushed inside to pack while Bobber jumped on his bike to ride home and get ready. I stopped to look at the map of the United States on my wall just to get a feel for where Louisiana was in relation to White Bear Lake, Minnesota.

I had just finished packing when Bobber's parents dropped him off. He walked in carrying a suitcase that looked like it was going to burst. It was more round than square and had clothes sticking out the sides. His favorite fishing hat was wrapped around the handle.

"Gee, Bobber, you didn't have to bring everything you own," I said, pointing to the ruler sticking out from among the clothes.

"That's my new FishingKids fish measuring ruler," he said proudly while stuffing it back into the side of the bag. "I also have a flashlight, a compass, and a bag of Atomic Fireball candy. I'm going to catch a fish so big we have to use three rulers to measure it!"

"Well, you might want to put some clothes in that bag, or else you're going to be wearing the same stuff every day. By the end of the trip, we'll be measuring how far we have to stay away from you in order to breathe," I said with a smile.

"I know. I know," said Bobber. "I was so excited I even packed the sandwich I was eating. If I hadn't have seen mustard squeeze out the side of my suitcase when I shut it, it would still be in there."

We both laughed, grabbed our bags, and headed for the door. As we passed my mom and dad's room, I saw two more suitcases next to the door.

"Spinner, did you pack everything you own?" asked Bobber.

"Those aren't my suitcases. My mom grew up in Louisiana, so she and my dad are coming, too," I told Bobber. "This is going to be the best fishing trip ever!"

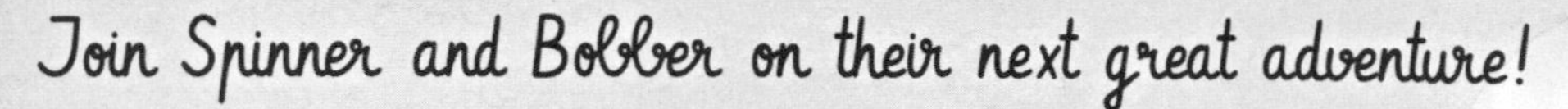

The boys are heading to Cajun Country, where they meet a new friend named Shrimp. It's a tale of pirates, gators, sunken treasure, and fishing fun. You won't want to miss FishingKids Book #3: The Pirate of Creole Bay.

The Pirate of Creole Bay

Available now at ...

www.FishingKids.com

Action Figures

Fishing Vests

Life Vests

FiSHiNG KiDS .com

Visit us online for games, fishing tips, and merchandise!

www.FishingKids.com

HOME PLAY LEARN EXPLORE SHOP

click here for a FREE BOOK!

Welcome

to the world of Spinner + Bobber

Get your FREE Book

Learn More

Play

Get ready for some online fun, with FishingKids games and coloring pages.

Explore

Learn about the FishingKids cast of characters & about fishing all across the U.S.A.

Shop

Visit Spinner & Bobber's Bait Shop for FishingKids books, toys, clothes, and more!

Join Spinner + Bobber as they share their fishing adventures from around the U.S.A.!

Meet Spinner and Bobber and discover the world of FishingKids. Our heroes — together with their parents, grandparents, and friends — travel across the country and get hooked on fishing and outdoor fun.

From chapter books and action figures to life jackets, compasses, and clothing...FishingKids has something for every young angler.

Check out our action figures & clothing

Get shopping! →

Now Available

FishingKids Book 2: *The Mystery of Porpoise Point*

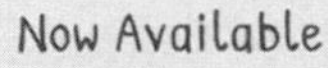

Read an Excerpt →

Order now! →

 PRIVACY POLICY CONTACT US

Polo Shirts

Shoe Bait

T-Shirts & More

Mike Holliday has been a USCG licensed fishing guide out of Stuart, Florida, since 1986. He has served in editorial positions with *Florida Fishing Weekly* and *Florida Sportsman Magazine*. A renowned writer and photographer, Mike is the author of three books on inshore fishing. His writing and photography credits also include *The Miami Herald, The Palm Beach Post, The Fort Pierce Tribune, The Stuart News*, and several other local and national fishing publications.

As a fishing guide, Mike targets trophy `snook, spotted seatrout, redfish, permit, tarpon, and flounder on the Treasure Coast. Adept at leading spin, plug, and fly anglers to the catch of a lifetime, he regularly pursues his targeted species in the Indian and St. Lucie Rivers and the nearshore waters of the Atlantic Ocean.

Mike currently resides in Stuart, Florida, with his wife and three children, where they are constantly on the water and living the dream.